RiverStream Reade
Great Reading • Real Learn

# Mouse

By Wendy Perkins

# RiverStream Readers
### Great Reading • Real Learning

## Pre1

**Learn to Read**

Frequent repetition of sentence structures, high frequency words, and familiar topics provide ample support for brand new readers. Approximately 100 words.

## 1

**Read Independently**

Repetition is mixed with varied sentence structures and 6 to 8 content words per book are introduced with photo labels and picture glossary supports. Approximately 150 words.

## 2

**Read to Know More**

These books feature a higher text load with additional nonfiction features such as more photos, timelines, and text divided into sections. Approximately 250 words.

Accelerated Reader methodology uses Level A instead of Pre 1. We have chosen to change it for ease of understanding by potential users.

Amicus Readers hardcover editions published by **Amicus**. P.O. Box 1329, Mankato, Minnesota 56002 www.amicuspublishing.us

U.S. publication copyright © 2012 Amicus. International copyright reserved in all countries. No part of this book may be reproduced in any form without written permission from the publisher.

Series Editor — Rebecca Glaser
Series Designer — Heather Dreisbach
Photo Researcher — Heather Dreisbach

RiverStream Publishing reprinted by arrangement with Appleseed Editions Ltd.

Printed in the United States of America at Corporate Graphics in North Mankato, Minnesota.

Library of Congress Cataloging-in-Publication Data
Perkins, Wendy, 1957-
    Mouse / by Wendy Perkins.
        p. cm. – (Amicus Readers. Animal life cycles)
    Includes index.
    Summary: "Presents the life cycle of a mouse from mating and birth to adult. Includes time line of life cycle and sequencing activity"–Provided by publisher.
    ISBN 978-1-60753-157-9 (library binding)
    1. Mice–Life cycles–Juvenile literature. I. Title.
    QL737.R6P44 2012
    599.35–dc22
                                          2010035674

1 2 3 4 5 CG 15 14 13 12
RiverStream Publishing—Corporate Graphics, Mankato, MN—112012—1002CGF12

# Table of Contents

# A Life Cycle

A male and female mouse sniff and scurry through a field. They are looking for a place to make a nest for their babies. Soon a new **life cycle** will begin.

pup

breeding

4

adult mouse

The mice have been **breeding**.

Now they use dry grass and fur to make

a cozy nest under a log. It will help keep

their babies safe from **predators**.

Breeding

## Pups

The babies grow inside their mother. Three weeks after breeding, a litter of three to six babies are born. Baby mice are called pups. They can't see or hear. They have no hair on their bodies.

Breeding — Pups born 3 weeks after breeding

litter

pups

The mother and father mice keep the pups warm. The babies drink milk by **nursing** from their mother. They start to grow fur when they are three days old.

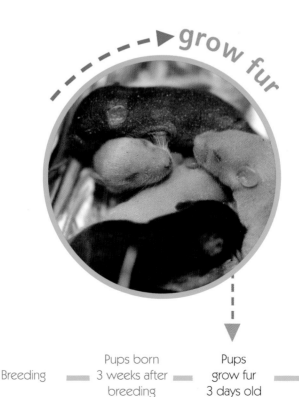

grow fur

| Breeding | Pups born 3 weeks after breeding | Pups grow fur 3 days old |

When they are ten days old, the pups can hear. At two weeks old, their eyes open and they begin to crawl. At first, they are very weak. As they move around, they grow stronger.

can hear

| Breeding | Pups born 3 weeks after breeding | Pups grow fur 3 days old | Pups can hear 10 days old |

eyes open

Pups' eyes open 2 weeks old

# Young Mice

At three weeks old, the young mice begin to feed themselves. They hunt for seeds and insects to eat. When it is time to sleep, they return to the nest.

| Breeding | Pups born 3 weeks after breeding | Pups grow fur 3 days old | Pups can hear 10 days old |
|---|---|---|---|

Pups' eyes open
2 weeks old

Feed themselves
3 weeks old

Mice leave their parents and can breed when they are seven weeks old. If they were born in the fall, they spend the winter in their parents' nest. When spring comes, they leave to find mates.

| Breeding | Pups born 3 weeks after breeding | Pups grow fur 3 days old | Pups can hear 10 days old |
|---|---|---|---|

Pups' eyes open 2 weeks old

Feed themselves 3 weeks old

Mice leave nest 7 weeks old

## Adults

It takes six months for a mouse to reach its full size. If a hawk or snake doesn't catch it, a mouse can live for two to three years.

| Breeding | Pups born 3 weeks after breeding | Pups grow fur 3 days old | Pups can hear 10 days old |

| Pups' eyes open 2 weeks old | Feed themselves 3 weeks old | Mice leave nest 7 weeks old | Full adult size 6 months old |

# Photo Glossary

**breed**
when a male and female join together to make babies

**life cycle**
the different stages of life from birth to having babies

**litter**
a group of babies born at the same time to one mother

**nursing**
to drink milk from a mother; mammals, including mice, nurse their young

**predator**
an animal that eats other animals

**pup**
a baby mouse

# Life Cycle Puzzle

The stages of a mouse's life are all mixed up.
Can you put them in the right order?

pups born

feeds itself

adult

breeding

building a nest

nursing

# Ideas for Teachers and Parents

Children are fascinated by animals, and even more so by life cycles as they grow up themselves. Books 1 through 5 in the RiverStream Readers Level 2 Series let children compare life stages of animals. The books use labels and a picture glossary to introduce new vocabulary. The activity page and time lines reinforce sequencing skills.

## Before Reading

- Read the title and ask children to tell what they know about babies or baby animals.
- Have children talk about whether they've seen mice before.
- Look at the picture glossary words. Tell children to watch for them as they read the book.

## Read the Book

- "Walk" through the book and look at the photos. Point out the time line showing how long mice spend at each stage.
- Ask children to read the book independently.
- Provide support where necessary. Show students how the highlighted words appear in the picture glossary.

## After Reading

- Have children do the activity on page 22 and put the stages of the mouse life cycle in order.
- Compare the life cycle of a mouse with other animals in the series. Does it have the same number of stages?
- Have children compare the human life cycle to a mouse's life cycle. How is it different? How is it the same?

# Index

# Web Sites

**American Fancy Rat and Mouse Association
(Kid's pages)**
http://www.afrma.org/kidskorner.htm

**Names of Animals, Babies, and Groups**
http://www.enchantedlearning.com/subjects/animals
/Animalbabies.shtml

Photo Credits
t=top; b=bottom; l=left; r=right; m=middle
Andrew Darrington /Alamy, 1, 17, 19; Eduard Kyslynskyy /Shutterstock, 15, 22tr;
IanCale/iStockphoto, 21m; J-L. Klein & M-L. Hubert/Photolibrary, cover, 4l, 4-5,
5, 7, 9, 11, 12, 13, 20t, 21b, 21t, 22tl, 22ml, 22bl, 22br, 22mr; Pierre Vernay/
Photolibrary, 10, 20b